Disney
✦ PRINCESS
Treasury

This is a Parragon Publishing book
This edition published in 2006

Parragon Publishing
Queen Street House
4 Queen Street
Bath, BA1 1HE, UK

ISBN 1-40545-974-3

Disney

✦ PRINCESS

Treasury

p

Contents

THE MICE SAVE THE DAY

Cinderella imagined herself dancing at the royal ball as she held her mother's old dress against her. It needed a few alterations, but they wouldn't be difficult, if only she could find the time to do them.

"Cinderellllaa!" yelled her stepmother and stepsisters again. They were getting ready for the ball and they wouldn't give Cinderella a moment's peace.

"I guess my dress will just have to wait," the poor girl sighed.

As she left the room, Jaq, one of Cinderella's favourite mouse friends, said, "Know what?

Cinderelly not go to the ball." The other mice looked at him, startled.

"Work, work, work!" he explained with disgust. "She never get dress done."

Cinderella's animal friends decided to surprise her by fixing the dress. After all, she had been caring for them for years. Just that day she had rescued poor Gus from a mousetrap. Then she had dressed him, fed him, and protected him from her stepmother's mean cat. So, together with the birds, her attic family lifted ribbons and scissors and sewing needles to help make

Cinderella's dream come true.

"Oh, thank you so much!" the beautiful girl

exclaimed when she saw what her friends had done

for her. The birds and mice were overjoyed to see
Cinderelly so happy. She deserved to have a special
evening. Never complaining for all she had to endure
from her stepsisters and stepmother, Cinderella still

hoped that one day she would find true happiness.

However, it was not long before her stepmother and stepsisters took hope away from her, too. Tearing her beautiful dress to shreds, they left her alone, sobbing in the garden.

"There, there," soothed a new voice. Cinderella's fairy

godmother magically appeared. "Dry your tears," she said. "You can't go to the ball looking like that."

Cinderella started to explain that she wasn't going to the ball, but her fairy godmother wouldn't hear of it.

Waving her magic wand, she turned a pumpkin into a

magnificent coach.

Cinderella and her animal friends stared at the

magic in amazement. "Bibbidi Bobbidi Boo!" sang the

fairy godmother. Soon, four of the mice, including Gus and Jaq, were turned into proud horses.

As for Cinderella, her new gown shimmered like diamonds. She stood staring at her image in the

fountain with disbelief.

"It's more than I ever hoped for!" she declared, her eyes sparkling.

When she arrived at the palace, Cinderella was swept into a dream world.

As she and the Prince swirled around the dance floor, everybody turned to stare at the beautiful girl who had caught the Prince's eye.

"Who is she?" they asked. "She must be a princess."

None could have imagined that earlier that day she

had been dressed in rags.

Never had Cinderella known such happiness! As the handsome young prince bowed before her, she felt her heart pounding. They danced together in the castle garden, swept up in the splendor of the evening.

Gazing into her eyes, the Prince leaned to kiss her just as the clock struck twelve. When she heard the bell toll, Cinderella remembered her fairy

godmother's warning that the spell would be broken
at midnight. She raced down the grand staircase,
leaving behind one of her dainty glass slippers.

The next day, doing her chores again, the young
girl hummed dreamily. Realizing that Cinderella was

the Prince's

mysterious

love, her

stepmother

mercilessly

locked her in

her attic room.

"No! Please let me out," cried Cinderella. She knew that the Grand Duke was trying the glass slipper on every maiden in the kingdom. He would be here soon.

"We've just got to get that key," Jaq told Gus. Despite the danger, they pulled the key out of the stepmother's pocket, then pushed and pulled it up the long staircase. With a last burst of energy, Cinderella's exhausted little friends were finally able to slip the

key under her locked door.

"Oh, thank you!" she cried.

Hurrying down the steps, Cinderella heard

a crash. The slipper she had left behind was broken! Pulling the other slipper out of her pocket, she called to the Grand Duke, "May I try this one on?"

The perfect fit proved that Cinderella was indeed the young woman who had won the Prince's heart.

Jaq and Gus cheered happily for their beautiful friend Cinderelly as they watched her dreams come true.

The Friendship of Fairies

In a magical kingdom there lived three kind and gentle fairies: Flora, Fauna, and Merryweather. Together, they worked to bring forth beauty, happiness, and love. Only by the power of their friendship could they defeat the evil power of their rival, Maleficent.

One day after Maleficent cursed the infant Princess Aurora with a powerful spell, the three good

fairies secretly conspired to protect the innocent baby. "Maleficent doesn't know anything about love or kindness or the joy of helping others," Fauna reminded her friends.

This thought gave Flora an idea. Maleficent would never expect them to live like peasants and raise the

child themselves. Fauna was overjoyed with the proposal, but Merryweather, being the practical one, was reluctant to give up her wand.

"We've never done anything without magic before," she complained. But Flora insisted that they could do it if they worked together.

With love, they cared for the beautiful princess as if she were their own daughter. For fifteen years they

kept her hidden in a

cottage in the woods.

Then, on the afternoon

before her sixteenth

birthday, the good fairies

sent Briar Rose, as they

had named her, to pick

berries so that they could plan a special surprise for

her. Although they were sad about returning her to

the King and Queen at sunset, they were content

thinking about her future happiness.

Aurora sang as she gathered berries. She had the

voice of an angel, and the squirrels and birds and other woodland animals came to listen. She told them her dream of meeting a handsome stranger and falling in love.

Nearby, Prince Phillip was riding his horse, Samson. Hearing Aurora's beautiful singing, he asked, "What do you think it is? A wood sprite, maybe?" He was so entranced by her song that he

promised Samson a carrot if he would follow the

music. Excited, the horse galloped too fast, knocking

his friend off into a stream.

"No carrots for you!" said the Prince.

Seeing the wet clothes, some rabbits and an owl decided to play a game with Briar Rose. Laughing, she danced with her make-believe stranger until she

realized that a
real man had
taken the place
of her
woodland
friends. As she
backed away,

Prince Phillip called after her, "But I'm not a stranger.
We've met before."

He reminded her of the song she had been singing:
"You said so yourself . . . 'once upon a dream.' "

Looking at him closely, Aurora felt that she really

did know him. His smile made her trust him, and she held his hand as they danced and walked through the magnificent forest. With a gentle touch and a tender look, they knew in a moment that this was a love as strong and true as one could ever be.

"This is the happiest day of my life," Briar Rose

proclaimed when she returned to the cottage.

However, Flora, Fauna, and Merryweather were not

pleased to hear about her handsome stranger. As they

explained that she was a princess, Aurora fell into

despair. She thought that she would never see her love again.

Sadly, the fairies led the Princess to her castle home, but they didn't realize that Maleficent had discovered them and was waiting to carry out her curse. As Aurora pricked her finger on the spindle of the spinning wheel and the whole castle fell into a deep

sleep, the good fairies realized that only the kiss of

true love would awaken the sleeping beauty.

Upon discovering that Prince Phillip was the

stranger that Aurora had met in the woods, they raced to Maleficent's castle and rescued him from her dungeon. The three fairies combined their powers of goodness in a fatal blow to the evil Maleficent. "Sword of truth, fly swift and sure, that evil die and

good endure." Their spell, combined with Prince

Phillip's strength of heart, put an end to the ferocious

dragon that Maleficent had become.

Awakened by a tender kiss, Princess Aurora

opened her eyes to behold the face of her true love.

As Princess Aurora and Prince Phillip expressed their

love to the kingdom, the fairies danced with pleasure – knowing that their beautiful Briar Rose would live happily ever after.

WALT DISNEY'S

Snow White
and the Seven Dwarfs

FRIENDS TO COUNT ON

Snow White glanced around her. It was very peaceful in the thicket and the sun was shining in the blue sky. It had looked different at night. She had been so afraid!

"What do you do when things go wrong?" Snow White asked the woodland  animals who had come to gaze at the lovely princess.

As the birds began to sing she joined them. Singing always made her feel better. Then she asked the animals if they knew of a place where she might stay. They led Snow White to a clearing where she noticed a charming little cottage.

When Snow White entered there was no one home. The room was dirty with dishes piled high in the sink and clothes tossed about. As she counted the adorable little chairs at the table, Snow White thought seven untidy children must live in this cottage.

Perhaps they have no mother, she thought sadly.

Deciding to surprise them by cleaning and making dinner, Snow White sang a cheerful song as she worked. The squirrels, chipmunks, deer, raccoons, and birds helped her dust, wash, and sweep. Snow White put soup on to cook, then climbed upstairs where she discovered seven little beds. Names were carved into each one: Doc, Happy, Sneezy, Dopey, Grumpy, Bashful, and Sleepy. What strange names for children, she thought, but the beds looked wonderfully inviting and she was awfully tired. As she lay across three of the small mattresses, the birds covered her tenderly

with a blanket, and Snow White fell fast asleep.

Soon seven dwarfs came home. "The whole house is clean!"

Doc

exclaimed.

Nervously

they tiptoed

upstairs.

Seeing a

large form under the sheets, they assumed it was a

monster and got ready to attack as Snow White began

to stir. Surprised, they stared at the beautiful girl.

"An angel," whispered Bashful, but Grumpy thought

differently. "All females are poison!" he insisted.

The nervous dwarfs hid behind the bed. The

Princess was startled as they peeked at her over the footboards. "Oh, you're little men!" she cried happily. Smiling, she guessed their names and explained how she had been sent away by her stepmother, the Queen. "She tried to kill me," Snow White told them, but Grumpy was unsympathetic.

"Send her away!" he yelled, nervous about the evil queen's black magic.

"She won't find me here," the Princess promised, "and I'll wash, and keep house, and cook . . ."

The dwarfs thought of the apple dumplings and gooseberry pies that Snow White could make. "She stays!" they agreed. Happily they followed her downstairs as she went to check on the soup.

"Wash up or you'll not get a bite to eat!" said Snow White as she checked their dirty hands.

Although the dwarfs dreaded soap and water, they wanted to make the Princess happy.

After dinner they played music and danced. Even

Grumpy played the pipe organ. Never had they had so much fun or laughed so hard!

"Now you do something," they urged Snow White. She began to tell them a story about a princess who fell in love. "Was it you?" they asked, and she nodded, remembering the charming prince who had appeared as

she was singing at a wishing well. Startled, Snow

White had run into the castle, but when the Prince

serenaded her, she looked out on the balcony. "He

was so romantic," she told her new friends. She had

sent him a kiss on the wings of a dove.

Sighing dreamily, the dwarfs gave Snow White their cozy beds for the night. Even Grumpy was happy that she had stayed.

"I'm warnin' ya . . . don't let nobody or nothin' in the house!" he said the next morning as he left for work.

"Why, Grumpy, you do care!" Snow White smiled as Grumpy stomped away. Then she kissed Dopey tenderly and sent him on his way.

Forgetting Grumpy's warning, Snow White allowed a poor old woman into the house that afternoon. The old woman offered her an apple, and not suspecting that it was the Queen in disguise,

the poor girl took one bite of the poisoned apple and fell to the floor.

Sadly, the dwarfs and forest animals grieved for their beloved princess until the day a prince appeared, having heard the story of a lovely girl in a glass coffin.

Recognizing her as the Princess he'd been searching for, he kissed her.

Slowly, Snow White awakened.

The happy prince

lifted her in his arms as the dwarfs and animals rejoiced around them. Cheerfully giving each of her friends a good-bye kiss, Snow White turned to her true love. As the birds sang, the happy couple walked toward a golden castle, where they lived happily ever after.

Walt Disney's Aladdin

THE PRINCESS WHO DIDN'T WANT TO MARRY

Princess Jasmine giggled with her friend Rajah. Although Rajah was a tiger he had always been her closest friend. Now he held a piece of Prince Achmed's pants in his mouth. He and Jasmine were both glad to be rid of the selfish suitor.

Jasmine's father, however, was not amused. "The law says you must be married to a prince by your next birthday."

Jasmine thought the law was unfair. She wanted to marry for love. "Try to understand, I've never done a thing on my own," she explained. Lately she wished that she were not a  princess at all. She felt as trapped as the caged doves.

That night the princess disguised herself, planning

to escape. As she began to climb over the palace wall, Rajah tugged on her dress. He was sad to see Jasmine leave, but knew what was best for her. "I can't stay here and have my life lived for me," she explained sorrowfully.

In the marketplace, life was busy and exciting.

With compassion, Jasmine handed an apple to a poor

child. However, when she was unable to pay, the

vendor grabbed her angrily. Luckily, a handsome

stranger came to her rescue. Running swiftly, they

escaped to his rooftop home.

Jasmine was thrilled with the thought of such freedom. This young man had no one to tell him what he could or couldn't do. As she was imagining his carefree life, the man looked longingly toward the

palace. It would be wonderful to live there, he thought, without having to worry about where to find his next meal.

"Sometimes I just feel so trapped," they both expressed at the same time.

Surprised, they looked at each other. Feeling a deep bond with this handsome stranger, Jasmine

leaned to kiss him, when suddenly guards burst upon them. There was nowhere to escape.

"Do you trust me?" asked the young man, holding out his hand to her. She looked into his brown eyes and placed her fingers in his grip. Quickly, they jumped off the tall building, their fall broken by a pile of hay. "I've got

you this time, Street
Rat!" yelled another
guard.

Jasmine revealed
herself as a princess
but they still arrested
her friend. "My orders
come from Jafar," the
guard told her.

Back at the palace,
Jasmine confronted her father's chief advisor. The evil
Jafar cruelly deceived her into thinking that her

handsome stranger was dead. "Oh, Rajah," she wept, as the tiger tried to comfort her.

Many days later, on the streets of Agrabah, there was a magnificent parade. Princess Jasmine, still

grieving, watched from her balcony. Trumpets were blaring, animals were doing tricks, fireworks blasted, but most impressive was Prince Ali, sitting on top of an enormous elephant, throwing gold coins into the crowd. Jasmine shook her head in disgust. Did he think he could buy her hand in marriage?

With anger, she yelled at the prince, "I am not a prize to be won!" But Prince Ali would not give up.

That evening he appeared on her balcony. Rajah growled protectively and was about to chase him away but Jasmine thought he looked familiar. She stepped closer and he showed her his magic carpet. "We could get out of the palace . . . see the world,"

Prince Ali offered.

Jasmine hesitated until he leaned forward offering his hand. "Do you trust

me?" he asked, and immediately Jasmine knew this was the same stranger she had met in the marketplace. Eagerly she climbed aboard and the carpet took them into the star-filled sky. Never had she seen such wonders! As they flew, she felt happier than she ever had before. Leaning on Prince Ali's shoulder she held his hand, not wanting the romantic night to end.

Unfortunately, Jafar soon discovered Prince Ali's magic lamp. He revealed Jasmine's love to be Aladdin, a poor boy from Agrabah. He had used a wish from the genie in the lamp to transform himself

into Prince Ali.

"Jasmine, I'm sorry I lied to you about being a prince," said Aladdin humbly. Jasmine held

his hands. She didn't love him for being a prince. She loved him for himself. Even the Sultan realized that Aladdin was worthy. When her father changed the law to allow his daughter to marry the man of her choice, Jasmine said, "I choose Aladdin." As fireworks lit the sky and the Genie and Abu waved good-bye, Aladdin and Jasmine shared a kiss on their magic carpet. Beneath them was a whole new world where they would live together, happily ever after.